D0500984

THE CHRISTMAS ELVES

by Henriette Major

Illustrated by Stéphane Poulin

Translated from the French by Alan Brown

Les lutins de Noël
Original edition

The Christmas Elves
Translation by Alan Brown

This translation was completed with the assistance of the Canada Council.

Canadian Cataloguing in Publication Data

Major, Henriette, 1933–
[Les lutins de Noël. English]
The Christmas elves

Translation of: Les lutins de Noël.
ISBN 0-7710-5473-4

I. Poulin, Stéphane. II. Title. III. Title:
Les lutins de Noël. English.

PS8576.A52L8813 1988 jC843'.54 C88-094355-6
PZ10.3.M335Ch 1988

Typeset by VictoR GAD studio
Printed and bound in Canada

McClelland and Stewart
The Canadian Publishers
481 University Avenue
Toronto, Ontario
M5G 2E9

It was fall, and Bing the elf was very upset. This was the time for harvesting his Christmas-tree balls, but there seemed to be very few of them this year. First it had rained and rained, and the balls couldn't start growing. Then the sun had come out and its burning light had dried the tender decorations until many of them crackled and broke in the heat.

Never, thought Bing. There'll never be enough for all the Christmas trees around here!

He picked all the balls that were left on their branches, piled them carefully in baskets, and went off to see how his neighbour, an elf called Bong, was doing.

Bing, you see, had a big plantation of Christmas-tree ball bushes, and his neighbour Bong had a splendid garden where he grew little coloured light bulbs, also for Christmas trees.

As everybody knows, Christmas-tree balls grow on bushes like raspberries, but the little lights grow on short plants near the ground, like strawberries. A very delicate kind of fruit.

"Just look!" said Bong. "My light bulbs have suffered from the weather too. They were soaked by the rain and they're all pale, they hardly give any light. I won't get many good ones this year."

Bing and Bong were good businessmen, so they started writing numbers on pieces of paper. They discovered that the bad weather had spoiled 10,456 ball decorations and 15,874 light bulbs. Thousands of customers were going to be disappointed.

"We have to do something," said Bing. "We can't leave all those Christmas trees standing bare."

"You're right," said Bong, "the world is sad enough without bare Christmas trees."

"Listen! I have an idea. We had a poor harvest here, but maybe lots of decorations grew Somewhere Else. Why don't we go there and have a look?"

“Good idea!” shouted Bong. “Who knows, maybe in some far-off southern countries we’ll find new kinds of decorations and light bulbs for Christmas trees.”

So Bing and Bong decided to go Somewhere Else. It happened that a flock of wild ducks were flying by, and Bing and Bong asked their friend the butterfly to take a message to the flight leader.

A few minutes later a sturdy duck landed near them, and Bing and Bong boarded flight 001 on its way to Somewhere Else. They were so thrilled that they began to sing a song, made up as they flew along.

Come along, Bing
Let's hear you sing
A good loud song
With no notes wrong
Bing bong!

It's your turn, Bong
To sing our song
In your squeaky voice
With words so choice
Singing bing bang bong.

The duck was an experienced flyer who knew his way around the sky. He flew so cleverly and fast that three days later Bing and Bong arrived in the land of Somewhere Else. The landing field was a beautiful yellow beach where the little waves of the Caribbean sea came lapping at their feet.

The first thing Bing and Bong noticed was the smell of flowers and spices in the air. They followed the perfume and soon came to a very strange garden. Bushes planted in even rows bore the most beautiful Christmas-tree balls you ever saw. Some were striped, some had polka dots, some had squiggles, and some were splashed with many colours. And there were Christmas-tree light bulbs too, in unusual shapes and colours. Bing and Bong could hardly believe their eyes.

They followed a path which soon led them to a pretty little bamboo house. And what a surprise when they saw on the verandah two little elves just like themselves, except that their skin was orange, not blue like the skin of Bing and Bong.

They said hello and told each other what their names were. Their new friends were called Ping and Pong; and when they found out that Bing and Bong were Christmas-tree decoration farmers, they invited them for lunch.

Soon Ping and Pong and Bing and Bong became good friends. Later they started talking business. They agreed to trade balls and light bulbs between the North and South. They were sure that people in the cold northern countries would love to use the brightly coloured decorations from the south, and the people from Somewhere Else would like to try pale, northern colours on their trees for a change.

To celebrate the deal, as well as their new friendship, the four elves did a little dance together that might have been a rumba or might have been a samba:

In our trees at Christmas time
Silver Christmas bells will chime

You'll hear Bing, Bong,
Ping, Pong
Sing all day long!

Very pleased to have solved their problem, Bing and Bong stayed on with Ping and Pong for a few days of lazy holiday time on the beach. Their blue skin quickly began to turn orange in the hot sun. They would have liked to stay longer, but Christmas was coming and they had to get back to work. It was time to go home.

First they had to see about getting the "Somewhere Else" Christmas-tree balls and light bulbs back to their northern home. But how? It was winter, and the ducks didn't fly north till spring. So they decided to use ocean travel.

To protect their breakable balls from the water, the two elves, Ping and Pong, got busy and made some waterproof boxes.

Then they found a friendly whale who carried their boxes to the northern lands, giving Bing and Bong a chance to do a little scuba diving.

Back on solid land again, Bing and Bong did some moose hiking. The adventurous monster brought them and their load of boxes right back to their farms.

From there the decorations were sent out to all the good stores in the towns and villages nearby. Soon the shelves were filled with balls and Christmas lights from the beautiful country of Somewhere Else, and customers flocked to buy them.

That year the Christmas trees in the region were magnificent, thanks to the decorations from Somewhere Else. Bing and Bong were proud of their clever idea.

Even now, in our times, Bing and Bong are famous for growing and importing the most beautiful Christmas-tree decorations ever seen.